Legacy of the Lightbearer
The Spirit Prince

Jay Thornton

A GOSHEN PUBLISHERS BOOK   VIRGINIA

Legacy of the Lightbearer
The Spirit Prince

ISBN: 978-1-959702-33-7
Copyright ©2025 Jay Thornton

Library of Congress Cataloging-in-Publication Data

Published in 2025 by:

GOSHEN PUBLISHERS LLC
10307 West Broad Street, #198
Glen Allen, VA 23060
www.GoshenPublishers.com

Our books may be purchased in bulk for promotional, educational, or business use. For inquiries please contact the publisher via email: Agents@GoshenPublishers.com.

First Edition 2025

Cover designed by Goshen Publishers LLC

Printed in the United States of America

For the dreamers who dare to imagine tomorrow—
May your courage shape the worlds yet to come.

Prologue:
The Warrior and the Flame

In the land of Kan'Moro, where spirit and soil breathe as one, legends are born not of crowns, but of sacrifice. And at the heart of the greatest legend was a prince—Jacques, heir to the Chui Leopard Tribe. His name was whispered by the wind, spoken with awe by the innocent he protected.

Born beneath a moonlit eclipse, Jacques carried more than noble blood. He bore the sacred powers of light, wind, heaven, and earth—gifts bestowed by the all-knowing Elohim, the Spirit of the Great Beyond. A warrior of the spirit, chosen not only to wield might, but to guard those who could not guard themselves. Wherever injustice crept, Jacques followed. With the wind at his back and light in his hands, he became a myth in motion—a protector, a prince, a beacon. But even the strongest light casts a shadow of longing.

In the heat of conflict and tribal tension, Jacques encountered Chausiki, the fierce and luminous princess of the Dumaja Cheetah Tribe. Her grace was unmatched, her speed untouchable, her spirit ablaze. She was raised to see Jacques as a rival. He was trained to see her as a threat. And yet, when their eyes met across a bloodless battlefield, something ancient stirred.

Their love did not bloom in peace. It was forged in silence and secrecy, in stolen moments beneath spirit-touched trees, in quiet oaths sworn beneath starlight. It was the kind of love the tribes forbade—the kind that could heal a broken world or destroy what little peace remained.

Kan'Moro teetered on the edge of war. The Azuuriic Lion Tribe, cunning and cruel, had allied with the ruthless Quaamati

Jay Thornton

Hyena Clan. Together, they moved like a shadow across the land, seeking to conquer not just territory, but spirit itself. Their armies grew stronger, their ambition bolder. And so, Jacques and Chausiki were left with a choice: to surrender to the ancient hatred that divided them—or to defy it. To unite their tribes not through force, but through love. To face the storm hand in hand.

This is the story of how a warrior and a flame risked everything to become more than legend. This is the story of how love became the greatest weapon of all.

Chapter One:
The Meeting of Light and Flame

The grasslands of Kwanza Ridge trembled beneath the thundering of feet. The warriors of the Chui Leopard Tribe surged forward with precision and strength, their bronze weapons glinting under the noonday sun. At their front, Jacques cut through the dust like a windstorm incarnate—his cloak whipping behind him, his eyes blazing with the light of the Great Beyond. Earth bent to his steps. The wind curved to his command.

Opposite him, the Dumaja Cheetah Tribe launched their counterstrike with agile ferocity. Moving like golden fire, they weaved through the battlefield with speed and silence. At their center, leading without hesitation, was Chausiki—her twin blades whirling with deadly grace, her voice carrying across the plains like thunder.

They met in the heart of the fray. Jacques saw her coming before the others. The way the wind parted for her. The way the light seemed to favor her stride. Their auras clashed before their blades ever could. Steel rang. Sparks flew. Their weapons met once, twice, then paused.

Jacques narrowed his eyes, voice steady. "You're no ordinary warrior."

Chausiki spun, planting her foot with fierce precision. "And you're no ordinary prince."

Their auras flared again—light and wind colliding, earth trembling beneath them. Time slowed. Then something unseen swept across the battlefield. A wave of stillness. A pulse from the Spirit Realm. Jacques and Chausiki felt it deep within their bones. A presence. Ancient. Watching. Calling. Their weapons lowered. All around them, warriors froze in place, unsure why their hearts suddenly ached, why the spirit whispered so loudly in their ears.

Jacques stepped back. "This war… it's not the answer."

Chausiki's eyes searched Jacques's eyes. "Then what is?"

He extended his hand. "Meet me. Away from this. One day. One chance. For something greater."

She hesitated, then nodded. "At the Temple of Winds. Three nights from now."

With that, they turned away, each returning to their sides, each forever changed. Three nights later, beneath a moon half-veiled by the clouds, they met in the Temple of Winds, its white stone towers humming softly with ancient energy. There were no guards. No weapons. Only silence.

They stepped toward one another as the wind stirred the dust around their feet. Then it happened. Their spirit marks ignited. Light shimmered along Jacques' arms, golden and blinding. Chausiki's hands glowed with flames tinged with blue. The wind coiled between them, and the stone floor beneath them cracked with vines of living earth. They gasped in unison. And from the sky above, the stars seemed to draw closer.

Elohim's voice echoed. "You are two flames from the same divine fire. My breath is in both of you. Unite the tribes or all will fall."

Jacques reached for her hand. Chausiki took it without fear. Their journey had begun—not just of love, but of destiny. Together, they would change Kan'Moro. Or die trying.

Chapter Two:
The Secret Bond

The Temple of Winds faded into the distance behind them, but the memory lingered. Jacques stood at the edge of the cliff overlooking the sacred valley below, where the wind whispered through spirit-touched reeds. His mind echoed with Elohim's words. His heart pounded, not from battle but from her. Chausiki. Her presence had changed everything.

He returned to the Chui stronghold in silence, masking the turmoil within. His father, Mfalme, questioned nothing, content that the border conflict had quieted. But Jacques knew peace was a fragile illusion, and the fire that burned between him and the Dumaja princess could either forge salvation or spark a greater war.

Three nights later, beneath the veil of darkness, Jacques left his camp once more. Chausiki waited for him in the sacred Grove of Whispers, hidden deep within the neutral hills. Lanterns of spirit light floated between the trees, casting a gentle glow on their faces. She was seated near a stone basin filled with still water. As Jacques approached, she rose; silent, regal, and radiant.

"I didn't think you'd come," she said softly.

He stepped closer. "I couldn't stay away."

They sat together on the stone steps, the air warm and hushed. "I haven't told anyone," Chausiki whispered. "Not even my closest guards."

"Nor have I," Jacques said. "They wouldn't understand."

She turned to face him. "We were chosen, Jacques. Not just to love… but to lead. To heal."

"And that frightens me more than war."

Chausiki reached out, her fingers brushing his. "Then let's start with truth. With trust. Just you and me."

He took her hand. "You have both."

As they sat in silence, a gentle pulse of light rose from their clasped hands. Not fire, nor wind—something new. Something sacred. They leaned toward each other slowly, cautiously… and kissed. It was not rushed. Not born of urgency or rebellion. It was surrender.

In the days that followed, they continued to meet in secret. Beneath waterfalls, among hidden ruins, deep within spirit caves where their ancestors once prayed. They trained together, blending their powers, discovering new techniques, testing the limits of wind-born flame and radiant earth. Their bond deepened with each encounter. Their souls began to speak even when their mouths were silent. But with each night that passed, the danger grew.

Eyes began to watch as whispers stirred among the Dumaja. A Vodai scout of the Crocodile Tribe reported strange energy readings near the Grove of Whispers. And in the Chui stronghold, Mfalme summoned his son more frequently, watching him with eyes sharp as steel. Jacques knew they could not remain hidden much longer. But as he investigated Chausiki's eyes during one moonlit meeting, he made a vow: "No matter what comes, I choose you. Even if the world does not."

Chausiki smiled, tears in her eyes. "Then we stand together. As one."

And the Great Spirit listened as the winds began to shift.

Chapter Three:
Secrets Unleashed

The moon was high over the Grove of Whispers. Jacques and Chausiki lay together beneath the braided branches of the spirit trees, wrapped in the warmth of each other's presence. The wind was still. The stars blinked like guardians above them. It was here, in this sacred space, that their love had deepened—beyond training, beyond destiny. Here, they kissed like flame and wind, danced like moonlight and earth, spoke in tones only two souls could understand. But they were not alone. Otanu, Jacques' younger cousin, had followed his trail out of curiosity and concern.

Perched silently behind the trees, he watched in disbelief as Jacques pulled Chausiki close, their hands intertwined, their bodies pressed close in sacred embrace. Otanu's heart pounded. His voice dropped into a horrified whisper: "No... No! This is not allowed! This can't be allowed!" His face twisted. "The Spirit Prince of the Chui Leopard Tribe and the Princess of the Dumaja Cheetah Tribe are secretly dating and training together? Ugh... Dang it, Jacques, what are you thinking?" He backed away quietly, shaking his head. "I must tell his father and his mother. They're in charge. They'll know how to straighten him out."

And before sunrise, Otanu did just that. The next morning, Jacques and Chausiki returned to their respective lands after one more night of joy. Their hands had only just parted when voices rose in rage. At the Chui stronghold, Jacques stepped into the great hall to find his parents waiting. Mfalme's jaw was clenched. Queen Zahara stood beside him, arms folded, eyes blazing.

"Is it true?" Zahara asked.

Jacques tensed. "What have you heard?"

"That you've been sleeping with the Dumaja princess," Mfalme snapped. "Our enemy."

"She is not our enemy!" Jacques shouted. "She's different. She sees me—not the prince, not the title—me."

Mfalme's voice rose like thunder. "You will obey and stick with choosing a worthy woman of our tribe—not share trysts with the enemy!"

Zahara's voice was quieter but sharper. "You shame your name, Jacques. The future of the Chui depends on you."

As the room grew tense, a new voice cut in. Legadema, regal in her white and gold robes, stepped forward with narrowed eyes. "What you are doing is a travesty against this tribe. You and I were chosen to continue the royal bloodline of the Chui—not with some tramp from the Dumaja!"

Jacques turned to her, fierce but steady. "I choose her. And no one else." He turned and walked out—out of the hall, out of the stronghold, and out of the Chui lands.

Meanwhile, in the Dumaja palace, Chausiki stood firm as her parents confronted her. "You were promised to Athuman," her father growled. "You disgrace our name."

"I never agreed to that promise," she said. "And I never will."

Her mother, eyes tight with sorrow, added, "Chausiki, you risk igniting war."

"For the last time," she said, her voice trembling with emotion, "I will not marry someone I don't love! I am in love with Jacques, the Spirit Prince of the Chui—and I stand by it."

With tears in her eyes, she turned and ran. Back at the Grove of Whispers, Jacques stood alone until the wind shifted. Chausiki appeared breathless, her cheeks wet with tears. Without hesitation, he ran to her, gathering her in his arms.

"They know," she whispered. "They all know."

"I know," Jacques said, cupping her face. "But you're safe with me." He dried her tears with gentle fingers and nuzzled her brow. "I'm not letting them take this from us."

Chausiki kissed him long, deep, and full of the pain and passion they carried.

But from the shadows, someone watched. Athuman's hands were clenched, eyes seething with betrayal. "I am going to challenge you, Jacques," he muttered, teeth grinding. "You'll see." And then he vanished back into the dark.

Jay Thornton

Chapter Four:
Fire in the Heart

Jacques and Chausiki walked hand in hand into Dumaja Territory. Their steps were steady, proud, defiant. The sun cast long golden rays across the village meeting center, but all eyes turned toward them in stunned silence. Warriors dropped their practice weapons. Elders paused their chants. Children stopped mid-play.

They made no effort to hide their unity as a couple. Their fingers were locked. Their chins lifted. Love and power walked beside them. At the steps of the stone dais, Chief Kosan stood with arms crossed and a thunderous gaze. Beside him, Matriarch Imani held her silence, her face tight with disdain.

Chief Kosan's voice boomed. "How dare you bring him here! A filthy Chui! He does not belong among us! Guards! Restrain them both and execute the Chui prince!"

"No! Father, stop! Let me go!" Chausiki cried.

As the guards rushed forward, Jacques and Chausiki moved in harmony. Blades met fists. Wind pushed bodies. Fire flared. In moments, the guards were unconscious, and the couple stood back-to-back, steady in stance and soul.

Chausiki turned to the people of her tribe, her voice cutting through the growing uproar. "I don't care what you all think! The Spirit Prince… my Jacques… is the one I love! I chose him, and he chose me—and I am more than happy to show you without hesitation." She turned, pulled Jacques close, and kissed him passionately. Their spirit energy flared as light, wind, and flame glow so golden and violet in radiance, curling around them like a protective cocoon. When they separated, breathless and blushing, their foreheads rested against one another.

Then a voice roared from the gathered crowd. "Enough!" Athuman stepped forward in full combat regalia, fury radiating from every motion. "You defy your tribe for him? Then I claim my right, by tradition and honor. I challenge you, Jacques of the Chui, for the hand of Chausiki!"

Jacques slowly turned, stepping forward as Chausiki reached for his arm. He looked into her eyes. "I'll end this."

The circle cleared. The drums fell silent.

Athuman lunged with brutal precision, swinging his obsidian blade. Jacques met him strike for strike, his body flowing like wind, each motion a dance of balance and intent. Steel clashed. Sparks flew. Their energies collided and rippled across the battlefield. With a sudden twist, Jacques shattered Athuman's chest plate with a burst of spirit-imbued light. The armor cracked, pieces falling to the dust.

"What?! No! I will not lose to a Chui!" Athuman screamed. "Now do me a huge favor and die, already!"

He wildly swung. Jacques ducked beneath the strike and rose in one fluid motion delivering a spinning roundhouse kick to Athuman's head. The warrior crashed to the ground, stunned.

Jacques stood over him with a blade composed of tungsten and steel edges. The blade pressed close to Athuman's neck. But as the crowd held its breath, Jacques decided not to kill him. He spoke with a voice calm and clear.

"If we continue this path, we will all be no more. Dumaja or Chui, none of it will matter. We must unite the tribes and reconcile with the others. The true enemy, the Azuuriic and Quaamati, wait for us to fall apart. We cannot face them if we are at war with each other."

Chausiki moved beside him, placing her hand on his. "Elohim has told us once," she said, "that every life spared and

Jay Thornton

not taken is a life that can be redeemed. Let's prove that to them by fighting together, all as one." She turned to the crowd, eyes shining with tears and power. "Sasa ni wakati wa sisi kuja pamoja kama moja! Sasa ni wakati wa hatima yetu mpya kufunua! Now is the time for us to come together as one! Now is the time for our new destiny to unfold!"

And in the silence that followed something began to change.

Chapter Five:
The Spirit Accord

The Grove of Whispers had never held so many voices. From every corner of Kan'Moro, tribal envoys and respected elders gathered beneath the ancient spirit trees, whose leaves shimmered like silver tongues in the morning light. The winds were hushed in reverence, and the ground pulsed with an energy that whispered of change. At the center stood Jacques and Chausiki, unshaken, side by side bruised from battle, but radiant in the glow of unity.

Their hands were clasped before the sacred circle, where ancient sigils glow faintly around a massive, floating spiritstone. The Chui had arrived as well as the Dumaja. Even the Vodai and Mhatu tribes sent scouts and seers, curious to witness the ones chosen by Elohim. From the high cliffs overlooking the grove, Mfalme, Jacques' father, watched in brooding silence. His jaw was tight, but his eyes betrayed awe.

Beside him, Queen Zahara gripped his arm gently and whispered, "Do you see it now? What was he born to do?"

Mfalme did not answer, but he remained. The spiritstone pulsed. A voice filled the grove—not loud, yet unmistakable. Deep, warm, and ancient. "Children of Kan'Moro… My breath moves among you." It was Elohim. "In your hearts, I planted seeds. In your union, I breathed a new flame. You were not meant to war forever. This is the moment to choose light over legacy. This is the moment to become one."

Silence fell as the Spirit Prince stepped forward. Jacques then raised his voice. "We stand not only as Chui and Dumaja— but as brothers and sisters of Kan'Moro. For too long, we've bled while the real enemy waits to strike. The Azuuriic and the

Quaamati gather their strength even now. We must be more than a rebellion. We must be a bond—formed not by fear, but by purpose."

Chausiki stepped beside him. "We offer not dominance, but an alliance. Not subjugation, but unity. A Spirit Accord. One built on mutual respect, shared strength, and sacred trust." The elders murmured. Murmurs turned to voices. Voices to chants. One by one, tribal leaders stepped forward laying their blades and talismans upon the ground in agreement. Even Chief Mfalme descended from his high place, walking to the edge of the circle.

He looked at Jacques, long and hard. Then he laid his hand upon the earth. "Let the Chui be counted among this accord."

Jacques swallowed hard, nodding.

From above, the wind swirled into the shape of a great spiral; Elohim's symbol of unity. "So be it," the Great Spirit whispered. "Let the Spirit Accord rise." And in the hush that followed, all of Kan'Moro held its breath. The tribes had come together, and the future had just begun.

Chapter Six:
The Path of Judgment

The Spirit Accord had formed, but peace would not come without fire. As the dawn broke over the Grove of Whispers, a low hum stirred the ground beneath the assembled tribes. The spiritstone at the center pulsed once, then twice, and flared in radiant light. The sigils etched into the trees glowed with golden energy.

Elohim's voice returned. "The time has come. Your unity must be tested by action. The shadow gathers in the east and south—where the Azuuriic Lion Tribe and the Quaamati Hyena Clan raise their banners of conquest. They seek not justice… only domination."

Above the grove, the clouds parted, revealing a tapestry of golden light. Within it, a vision unfolded. A sweeping savanna filled with roaring flames and iron-clad lion warriors. A jagged canyon shrouded in darkness, where hyena assassins moved like smoke.

"These are the strongholds of your enemies," Elohim said. "They prepare for war while you speak of unity. Go now. Confront them not with hatred, but with purpose. Let your strength reveal the truth of your bond." As the vision faded, the warriors of the Spirit Accord prepared.

Jacques stood at the front; spirit-marked armor gleaming. Chausiki joined him, her blades newly etched with the Accord's crest—light woven with wind. He turned to their assembled force. "The Azuuriic and Quaamati do not believe we can stand together. They expect division. We will show them the strength of unity. Not with reckless slaughter, but with righteous defense."

Chausiki added, "We do not fight for vengeance. We fight to protect those they would crush. To offer even our enemies a chance at redemption."

The march began. Scouts were dispatched. Spirit channelers opened the old paths. Every warrior, whether Dumaja wind-runner or Mhatu sky-guard, carried the light of something greater. As the Spirit Accord moved out, the ground beneath Kan'Moro seemed to pulse with approval. The path to war had begun, but so too had the path to salvation.

Chapter Seven:
The Azuuriic Stronghold

The savanna was silent. The only sound was the whisper of wind brushing against steel as the Spirit Accord stood at the edge of the Ember Plains, gazing at the colossal fortress that rose like a sun-scorched mountain of gold and obsidian. The Azuuriic Stronghold. Lion banners rippled in the dry wind. Guard towers loomed; their watchmen clad in golden helms.

Spears tipped with sunstone glinted from every wall, and at its heart, a massive statue of the Azuuriic Warlord, Zuberi, glared across the plain with fire in his eyes. Jacques crouched beside Chausiki on a rocky ridge, studying the formation. "Their numbers are great. Their pride, greater."

"But their unity is hollow," Chausiki whispered. "They rule through fear—not spirit."

Behind them, the Spirit Accord leaders Jengo, Kisha, Naari, and several Vodai and Mhatu commanders, formed a half-moon around the couple.

Jacques rose and turned to the warriors. "This is not a siege. We are not conquerors. We strike to cripple their might, to show them what true strength looks like—strength born from unity."

Jengo pointed to the fortress's western edge. "There is a hidden aqueduct that runs under the structure. My channelers can breach it without detection."

Naari grinned. "I'll take a team in with them. Quiet and fast."

Chausiki nodded. "Jacques and I will lead the main charge from the east, after the diversion is triggered. That's when we break their gate—not just physically, but spiritually."

As night fell, the Spirit Accord moved. The moon rose high as Naari and her infiltration team slipped into the shadows. Spirit glyphs shimmered faintly across their armor as they vanished into the dried riverbed. At dawn, the first explosion sounded. The aqueduct erupted in a tower of steam and shattered stone. Alarms rang. Azuuriic guards scrambled into formation.

Then came the eastern charge. Jacques led the vanguard, his blade glowing with holy light. Chausiki followed with a windstorm at her heels. Warriors of every tribe surged behind them—Chui leopards roaring, Dumaja cheetahs flashing through enemy lines, Vodai spiritbearers shielding their flanks. Steel clashed. Spirit ignited. Jacques met Zuberi in the center courtyard.

The lion warlord towered over him; sun-forged armor ablaze. "You think unity makes you strong?" Zuberi growled.

Jacques raised his sword. "Unity is strength. And yours is built on fear." Their blades met in a crash of light and fire. Meanwhile, Chausiki danced through the chaos, disabling guards with bursts of wind and swift strikes. Her presence inspired awe even among their enemies. The fortress shook rapidly.

After a brutal clash, Jacques disarmed Zuberi, driving him to his knees. "Yield," he said, "and your people may yet have a future."

Zuberi looked at the warriors around him—Chui, Dumaja, Mhatu, Vodai—all fighting as one. He dropped his blade. The battle was won. The Azuuriic were broken. Not by destruction, but by revelation. As the Spirit Accord raised their banner above the fortress, a new wind swept across the savannah. And far away, deep in the canyons of the south, the Quaamati Clan began to stir. Their turn was next.

Chapter Eight:
The Howling Canyons

The canyons whispered with ghosts. Far from the sun-bleached savannahs of the Azuuriic lands, the Quaamati strongholds lay hidden deep within the cliffs of the Black Maw—a winding labyrinth of stone, darkness, and shadow. Here, the wind howled with the cries of past battles. The hyena clans thrived in secrecy, striking from the darkness, never leaving a trace. But now, their time in the dark was coming to an end.

Jacques, Chausiki, and the Spirit Accord stood at the mouth of the canyon, cloaked in shadow. The victory at the Azuuriic fortress had shifted momentum in their favor, but the Quaamati were cunning and their underground empire would not be broken by force alone. Kisha, the Mhatu scout commander, knelt beside a rock etched with blood-red glyphs. "They've rigged every entrance. Traps, spirit wards, echo signals. One misstep and the canyon will collapse on top of us."

Naari unsheathed her twin daggers, smirking. "Sounds like fun."

Jengo nodded, eyes scanning the cliffs. "We'll need silence and coordination. The Quaamati thrive on confusion. We counter it with clarity."

"We move in waves." Chausiki glanced at Jacques. "Naari and I lead the infiltration. You strike with the second wave when we breach the inner circle."

Jacques leaned closer, his forehead to hers. "Be swift, be safe. I'll be right behind you."

With a silent nod, the first group slipped into the shadows. The interior of the canyon was alive with flickering flames and eerie chants. Quaamati scouts lined the cliffs like spiders, watching, waiting. Spirit traps hung from stone arches—twisted charms of bone and whispering leaves. Naari's squad moved with silence, disabling alarms with Vodai-purified water, cutting ropes and glyphs before they could activate. Chausiki led them into the heart of the canyon, a ceremonial arena ringed by jagged obsidian pillars.

There, the Quaamati chieftain waited. Zavii, daughter of the High Fang, wore black armor crafted from bones and shadow-shaded steel. Her laugh echoed before she spoke. "You think you can slither into our den and not be torn apart?"

Chausiki stepped forward, blades drawn, aura burning with wind and spirit. "We didn't come to be torn. We came to end the cycle."

A whistle sounded. The battle erupted. Jacques led the second wave through a breached tunnel, light flaring in his hands as he brought down two cloaked hyena assassins in one breath. The canyon roared with combat. Spirit energies clashed like storms between cliffs. Jacques and Chausiki fought side by side, moving as one. Where he blocked, she struck. Where she faltered, he lifted. Zavii darted in and out of shadow, striking like a viper, but Chausiki met her blow for blow.

When Zavii leapt for a finishing strike, Jacques caught her mid-air with a shield of earth and wind. Disarmed and breathless, Zavii fell. Jacques stood over her. "You can surrender. Or fade like a whisper in the dark."

Zavii looked up, then dropped her blade. "I choose the light."

By nightfall, the Quaamati had fallen silent. The Spirit Accord's banners now stood in the heart of the canyon— symbols of peace in the place once known only for ambush and fear. And in the depths of the Spirit Realm, Elohim stirred. Though the armies of the present had been disarmed, an older enemy was awakening. One far more dangerous than the lions or the hyenas. One that remembered the First War.

Chapter Nine:
The Awakening Below

Night fell with an uneasy stillness. Though the banners of the Spirit Accord now flew over both Azuuriic and Quaamati strongholds, a strange tension rippled through the Spirit Realm. The winds felt heavier. The stars above Kan'Moro flickered with unnatural patterns. The Spirit Wells, once glowing steadily with Elohim's light, pulsed in irregular waves. Jacques sat alone in the Grove of Whispers, meditating beneath the ancient Spirit Tree. His connection to Elohim had always been a bond of clarity, but now, a storm brewed behind the veil.

Suddenly, light filled the grove. The Spirit Tree glowed from its roots to its crown. Jacques' body stiffened as his vision was pulled inward, past time, past form, past flesh. Elohim's voice emerged, deeper and more urgent than ever before. "The war of tribes was but a shadow of what lies beneath."

Images flashed before him. A massive gate carved in obsidian, buried deep within Kan'Moro's roots. Ancient beings wrapped in chains of fire and shadow, stirring in the dark. Spirit glyphs cracking. Forgotten names whispered by lost winds. "The First Ones... my first creations... rise once more." Jacques gasped as his vision returned.

Chausiki ran to him, sensing the surge. "What happened?"

He looked up, heart pounding. "They're waking up. Not the tribes. Not Erazion. The First Ones—those who came before the Guardians. Elohim says they've been sealed... until now."

Within hours, the council gathered. Chui, Dumaja, Vodai, and Mhatu all stood around the Great Spirit stone. Jacques and Chausiki explained the vision. Jengo stepped forward, face pale. "There are legends in Vodai texts… souls who have walked before the Spirit Wells. Banished for challenging the will of Elohim. Thought to be myth."

"They're no myth," Chausiki said. "And they're coming back."

Maps were unrolled. Spirit scribes deciphered fragments etched in forgotten dialects. The deepest Spirit Well, hidden in the ancient Vale of Orun'Dai, was marked. That's where the seal was weakening. A scouting party was formed, and a small force of elite warriors and seers would travel to Orun'Dai to find the truth. And prepare for what might be the greatest war Kan'Moro had ever faced.

As they rode out at dawn, the sky behind them wept light. Far below, in the deep chambers of the forgotten earth, the First Ones stirred. Their eyes opened and hunger returned.

Chapter Ten:
The Vale of Orun'Dai

The journey to Orun'Dai was unlike any the Spirit Accord had faced. Beyond the lush plains and mountain passes of Kan'Moro, past the forgotten ruins of the Mhatu and the mist-cloaked waters of the Vodai, lay the ancient Vale hidden, untouched, and wrapped in silence. No bird flew above it. No wind stirred its trees. The Vale of Orun'Dai was a place even the spirit winds feared to pass.

Jacques led the small company with Chausiki at his side, their steps deliberate as they moved through shadow and myth. Kisha, Naari, and Jengo followed closely, every one of them sensing the thickening spiritual current. Each night, Jacques's thoughts returned to Elohim's vision of the First Ones chained beneath the world, of their power beginning to rise. But one question echoed louder than all others: Was someone helping them awaken? At their campfire on the second night, Jacques sat quietly beneath a broken moon, eyes closed, hands pressed together.

"Elohim," he whispered, "if there is someone... if there is a will behind this awakening beyond the seal itself... show me. Give me a sign. I ask not from fear but from duty." The fire became dim and the air cooled. Suddenly, the flames surged with blue and white light, and a swirl of ash rose upward shaping into a spiral, then a serpent with three eyes. Jacques watched as it hissed silently, then burst into embers. He opened his eyes slowly. Chausiki approached.

"You saw something."

He nodded. "Not just a sign. A message. Someone is releasing them. And it's not just power... it's betrayal."

By the third day, they reached the outer edge of Orun'Dai. Massive stones jutted from the earth like jagged bones. Vines coiled like veins over collapsed temples. Strange glyphs glowed faintly along the cavern walls—a language not seen since the First War.

Jengo ran his fingers along one. "These were not sealed… they were ripped open from the inside."

Kisha knelt near a Spirit Well whose waters churned with black light. "Something's already been here."

"Then we're not alone." Naari unsheathed her weapons.

Jacques and Chausiki stood at the central dais, where an altar split in half now rested. A great chain hung from the sky above it severed and shattered. Beneath the earth, something growled. Not of flesh and not of a beast. But of a memory. And the First Ones were listening. Their return was no accident. And somewhere in the shadows of Kan'Moro, someone was unlocking the door. Jacques gripped his blade. "We must find out who… before it's too late."

Chapter Eleven:
The Betrayer in the Shadows

The ruins of Orun'Dai whispered louder with every step. Jacques, Chausiki, and the elite team pressed deeper into the broken heart of the Vale, guided by fading echoes of Elohim's presence and the gnawing certainty that something vile stirred beneath. Jengo paused near a collapsed arch. "There's a trail here… fresh. Someone's been moving through the inner sanctum recently."

Naari touched the earth. "It's not a beast. Human footprints. Heavy and deliberate."

They moved in silence, continuing deeper into the shadowed corridor until they reached a half-shattered door carved from black stone and rimmed in red. Behind it, the group could hear chanting. Jacques held up a hand, signaling quiet.

Through the cracks, they saw him. A man robed in charred crimson and bone-gray, his hands etched with glyphs of corrupted power. His face, once a family member to the Dumaja Tribe, twisted in darkness. Abuthos. A former tribal seer, thought to have vanished years ago. They watched as he knelt before a swirling black mirror embedded in the wall. A voice— terrible and familiar—echoed from within. Erazion.

"You have done well, my apprentice," the fallen spirit growled. "While those mortals fought each other, we have gathered power daily. Rise, Abuthos, and see how our Lord and Master, Hassatan, will dominate this land and then the entire planet." Erazion's laughter slithered through the air. Abuthos joined in, his voice giddy with corruption.

From the center of the black mirror, fire erupted. And from the pit of the Void emerged a figure of hatred wreathed in shadows and flame. A smile carved from malice spread across his face. Hassatan. The Dark Lord of Sheol.

"Has it all been done?" he asked, his voice like a thousand knives grinding together. "Have you devoured enough of the Light in this sector and turned it the Darkness?"

Erazion bowed. "Yes, my Lord. We have. And the mortals never even noticed."

Abuthos sneered. "Hah! Not even Elohim can stop us now!" He laughed madly until Hassatan raised a hand.

"Silence!"

Abuthos froze. "My sincerest apologies, Master Hassatan."

"Have you been followed?"

"No, my Master. I assure you that I was not followed."

Hassatan stired in approval and said, "Good... and from now on you will address me as Lord Hassatan. I am not a Master...yet."

Abuthos bowed deeply, trembling. "Yes, of course... of course..."

His flames pulsing, Hassatan turned to Erazion. "Have the Spirit Wells all been opened and remain untouched?"

Erazion nodded. "Yes, Lord Hassatan. My apprentice and I have done all you commanded and only what you command."

"Excellent," Hassatan hissed. "Because if either of you fail me, I will strip away your power and devour your souls instead." Both dark servants bowed lower, silent and terrified.

Outside the chamber, Jacques clenched his fists. "Elohim was right. This goes deeper than war. It's cosmic. Ancient. We're not just fighting to save tribes—we're fighting to protect all creation."

Chausiki nodded grimly. "And if Hassatan returns fully... nothing will survive."

In a whisper, Jengo warned, "We need to destroy the gate. Cut off their tether."

Naari added, "And expose Abuthos to the world. Let the Accord see the face of the true betrayer."

Nodding, Jacques stepped back, leading the group toward a secret path deeper into Orun'Dai. "We'll search every ruin, decode every glyph, find every tool we can. If we're going to face gods, we'll need more than just unity."

Chausiki took his hand. "We'll need faith."

From the shadows of Orun'Dai, a wordless whisper rose. The First Ones were watching, and they would not wait much longer.

Chapter Twelve:
Before the Gate Falls

The tunnels of Orun'Dai trembled. With the truth revealed and Abuthos' betrayal confirmed, Jacques and the Spirit Accord's elite force moved swiftly through the deeper chambers of the ruin. Echoes of Hassatan's voice still lingered in the stone, and every flame that flickered felt like eyes were watching their every move.

They had one goal now: destroy the black gate before it could open fully and let the First Ones pass into the world. Jengo led the way, spirit glyphs glowing on his palms. "I can sense the energy tether. Its root is in the altar chamber. If we shatter it, the gate collapses."

Kisha glanced behind them. "We won't be alone. That thing in the mirror knows we're coming."

Naari drew both blades, her voice tense. "Then we hit fast. In and out."

The corridor opened into a great underground sanctuary, its walls curved like a jawbone. The gate loomed at the far end—towering, pulsing with veins of red and black. Chains of corrupted spirit energy anchored it to the ground, glowing like lava. And there guarding it were corrupted guardians, spectral figures twisted by shadow, bearing the sigils of tribes long lost to time.

Jacques stepped forward, blade gleaming with Elohim's light. "Protect Jengo. Chausiki and I will hold the line."

The spirits swiftly charged. The clash was immediate as wind and flame battled against shadow and fang. Chausiki struck with bursts of blinding speed, her daggers weaving through the corrupted as Jacques summoned pillars of light and stone to push them back.

Jengo reached the altar. "Hold them!" He began his chant, calling down a column of pure spirit light. The energy crackled as the tether twisted and resisted. "Now!" he shouted.

Jacques and Chausiki unleashed their Spirit Form— wind, earth, light, and flame merging into a single radiant force. They struck the tether with Jengo's light. The altar shattered and the gate roared. It shrieked like a wounded beast as its surface cracked. Chains exploded into fragments of dark mist. The mirror of fire twisted in on itself, folding space as it screamed.

In the chamber beyond, Abuthos cried out. "No! You fools! You don't know what you've undone!"

Chausiki hurtled a bolt of compressed air at him, slamming him into a pillar. The gate collapsed in a thunderous implosion, pulling debris and howling wind into a vortex of fading corruption. Silence followed. The tether was broken. But Jacques turned toward the remnants of the gate.

"It wasn't the only one," he said, voice grim. "There are others."

Chausiki stepped beside him. "Then we find them. We stop this before it begins."

Far above, as they emerged from the Vale, the stars shifted. One blinked out. And in the distance, a second gate stirred. The war was only beginning.

Chapter Thirteen:
Across the Veins of Spirit

The sky above Kan'Moro shimmered strangely in the early morning light. Though the first gate had been destroyed, Jacques and Chausiki stood at the edge of the Vale of Orun'Dai with grim resolve. The stars told a new story now—one blinking out with each passing day. The Spirit Accord gathered once more.

Around them stood warriors, seers, channelers, and scouts from every tribe. Some were wounded from the last battle, but undefeated. Jacques raised his hand toward the rising sun. "The war has changed. The First Ones will try to rise again through any of the Spirit Wells still open."

Jengo stepped forward, scrolls of glowing ink in hand. "My seers have traced four known Spirit Wells with signs of gate activity. They're pulsing with unfamiliar currents… the seals are weakening."

Naari crossed her arms. "That many? We won't be able to hit them all at once."

"Then we divide, but not apart." Jacques placed a hand on Chausiki's shoulder. "She and I will take the southern path to the Sunken Temple beneath the Akari Sea. That's where I believe Erazion will strike next."

Chausiki added, "Jengo, you'll lead a team north toward the Echoing Peaks. Naari, take Kisha and sweep the desert ruins of Tir Zaan. We know Abuthos won't rest, and Erazion may already be preparing to use one of these gates to release Lord Hassatan." A hush fell over the camp as the weight of that name settled.

Jengo adjusted his staff. "What happens if he succeeds?"

Taking a deep breath, Jacques looked out over the savanna's plains. "Then light will die. And Kan'Moro will become nothing more than a path of ash to the rest of the world."

Chausiki held his hand. "We won't let that happen. Elohim chose us not to hold the line, but to forge a new one."

With goodbyes exchanged and maps shared, the Spirit Accord dispersed. Jacques and Chausiki rode south by spirit-beast and moonlight. Through jungle ruins and flooded plains, they drew closer to the Sunken Temple where whispers told of a well that was sealed. Not by stone, but by memory. Beneath the waves, ancient chains stirred. And Erazion... was already watching. His voice echoed through the realm of shadow: "You cannot stop what was written before the stars. And when the next gate opens, I will not be alone."

Chapter Fourteen:
The Temple Beneath

The Great Akari Sea was calm—too calm. As Jacques and Chausiki sailed across its black waters aboard a Spirit Accord skimmer, the horizon ahead faded into thick mist. Beneath them, waves broke gently over what legend called the Sunken Temple—an ancient sanctuary lost to time, built to hold one of the first Spirit Wells ever shaped by Elohim. And now, one of the last gates.

They dove together beneath the waves, guided by glowing spirit lanterns and enchanted breath-stones. The deeper they swam, the colder it grew, the current pressing against their bodies like invisible hands trying to pull them back. Then the temple appeared, an inverted pyramid of luminous coral, pulsing with light and shadow. The water surrounding it shimmered not with sun, but with the signs of the spirits. As their feet touched the ancient stone floor inside the temple, the sea seemed to vanish from around them. They stood in a pocket of preserved space; airless, yet breathable. Weightless, yet grounded.

Jacques drew his blade. Chausiki summoned wind into her hands. Then, the floor split. A creature surged from the chasm below; twisted and massive, its body formed from drowned spirits, chains of coral, and tendrils of living shadow. Its eyes glowed violet. Its voice was a blend of weeping and wrath. "You do not belong in this sanctum! Return to the surface or drown in your arrogance!"

Jacques stepped forward, his voice calm. "I am the Spirit Prince, and this temple belongs to Elohim." The beast roared and took a lunge at him, turning into a fight unlike any

Jay Thornton

before. Elohim's presence filled their minds and bodies, guiding their movements, amplifying their senses. Jacques spun with perfect precision, his blade flowing like a river of light through the corrupted tendrils. Chausiki moved in harmony, her wind forming shields and slashes that bent around the beast's defense. Each strike guided. Each breath, divine.

"Your unity is an illusion!" the creature hissed, slamming a massive claw into the ground.

But Jacques was already mid-leap. "Our unity is Elohim's will." He drove his blade deep into the core of the creature's chest as Chausiki channeled a spiral of wind and flame into the wound. Light exploded and the creature shrieked. Its form broke apart into mist, and then into nothing.

The chamber quieted and at the center of the temple, a crystal seal floated in mid-air. The gate stood, still dormant, still sealed. Jacques reached toward it, and Elohim's voice filled the space: "Well done, my children. One gate is saved. But the darkness does not rest. You must continue."

Chausiki took Jacques' hand. "This was only the beginning." Together, they turned away from the gate stronger in spirit, soul, and love. And far above, another star from the heavens blinked out, causing the next gate to stir. And the true war had only just begun.

Chapter Fifteen:
The Scattered Clues

While Jacques and Chausiki sealed the gate beneath the Akari Sea, the other Spirit Accord teams pressed into their missions across Kan'Moro's hidden places. Each one of them carried the weight of fate, uncovering pieces of a deeper, darker design. High in the Echoing Peaks, Jengo's team braved thin air and unstable cliffs. Snow fell in spirals, and strange songs echoed across the mountains.

Within a ruined temple carved into the rock, they found it: A fractured mural, ancient and divine, showing three great gates. One shattered, one dim, and one wide open. A shadow loomed beyond them, marked by the same spiral symbol etched into the core of the first Spirit Well.

Jengo narrowed his eyes. "This… this is not just prophecy. It's a warning." He traced a star map etched into the stone. "Each gate is aligned with celestial events. And at the center, beneath Kan'Moro itself, a hidden convergence."

In the desert ruins of Tir Zaan, Naari and Kisha moved like whispers through wind-swept rubble. Beneath a buried chamber, they discovered an obsidian monolith half-swallowed by sand. Kisha touched its surface and the monolith spoke. Not in voice, but through a vivid vision. A world wrapped in fire. A tower of flame rising from Sheol's core. Chains of the spirit world were burning away bit by bit. And the sun was fading away from the place they called home. Never to bring Elohim's warmth of light to rise again. At the peak stood a figure cloaked in darkness. His arms were spread wide while he laughed menacingly. It was Hassatan himself.

Naari pulled her back. "What did you see?"

Kisha whispered, "He's not trying to open the gates to cross into our world… he's trying to pull our world into his."

Back at the Spirit Accord's central camp, the teams reunited. Maps were unrolled, visions exchanged, energy patterns aligned. Jacques stood at the head of the circle; his jaws clenched. "If he succeeds in breaching all the wells, this world won't just fall—it'll merge with Sheol itself."

Chausiki added, "And from there, Hassatan will have access to the entire spiritual fabric. Every tribe. Every soul." Jengo tapped the central point on the map where all the ley lines converged. "Here. The Heart of Kan'Moro. A dormant Spirit Well hidden since the First War."

Jacques looked to the horizon. "Then that's where we go next."

Far beneath their feet, ancient chains began to strain. And somewhere in the deepest pit of Sheol, Hassatan opened his eyes. "So… they begin to understand."

Chapter Sixteen:
Vows Beneath the Stars

That night, as the Spirit Accord prepared for their final mission, a holy stillness settled over the land. The fires had dimmed, and the banners were folded. But the stars burned brighter than they had in generations. Jacques and Chausiki lay together in their tent, wrapped in each other's warmth, when a sacred light filled the space.

A voice soft, radiant, and infinitely echoed around them. "My children, you have done well." It was Elohim. "But know this: I am not only the one who gave you the spirit powers of light, wind, heaven, and earth. I am the Creator of all things. Of stars and silence, of life and eternity."

Jacques sat up, his breath held.

"You are not merely warriors. You are reflections of my divine hope. You are my covenant to the world."

And as quickly as the light appeared, it faded, leaving the two breathless and still. Plans were made that night. At first light, the Spirit Accord would march to the Heart of Kan'Moro. The final gate stirred beneath it, and all of creation now balanced on its seal. But as the camp slept, Jacques awoke. He rose quietly, pulled on a robe, and stepped outside. The cliff above the valley offered a panoramic view of the sleeping army below, warriors, leaders, and dreamers from every tribe. All united because of the love he and Chausiki refused to surrender.

Chausiki's voice broke his thoughts. "Why are you up? Aren't you sleepy?"

He turned to see her approaching in a flowing cloak, her hair catching the starlight.

Jay Thornton

Jacques smiled softly. "Yeah, but, Chausiki, I have something I need to tell you. It's very important."

She moved beside him, curious, and kissed his cheek playfully. "Yes, love? What is it?"

He took a breath, then stood tall. "I... I don't want our relationship, this deep bond we've grown, to end after the war. I want something more... something pure and true."

Chausiki gasped, her heart skipping. "Jacques... what are you saying?"

Jacques dropped to one knee, taking her hand in his. His spirit energy shimmered faintly around them like moonlight. "Chausiki, Princess of the Dumaja, my light in the dark... will you join me in holy matrimony, in both body and spirit? Will you join our souls as one?"

Tears welled in her eyes as she caught her breath. "Oh my... yes! My answer is yes! Of course, my Spirit Prince! I will marry you a thousand times over!"

They embraced one another as their spiritual souls ignited in a gentle flare of wind and fire. The pair shared a kiss that lasted throughout the night. Long, deep, and sacred. And in the sanctity of that moment, their love became more than a vow. It became a covenant, bound by divinity. They held each other passionately beneath the stars until the night grew quiet.

At dawn, they awoke in each other's arms, sharing a final moment of peace before rising. Dressed in full armor, they stepped forward together. The Spirit Accord awaited them from below. The path to the Heart of Kan'Moro stretched out ahead in one final journey to confront the rising doom, Hassatan. Hand in hand, they marched together as soulmates, warriors, and the last great hope of the world.

Chapter Seventeen:
The Heart of Kan'Moro

They arrived at dawn. The Heart of Kan'Moro lay hidden beneath a ring of stone ridges, shrouded in mist and glowing with ancient energy. It was a place untouched by war, sealed long ago in the days of the First Guardians. But now… it pulsed like a wound reopening. Jacques and Chausiki stood at the head of the Spirit Accord as the mist parted, revealing the sacred crater. At its center rose a spire of crystal-veined earth—an ancient Spirit Well, unlike any they had seen. Light radiated from its base, but it was fractured. Darkness crawled through its veins like ink in water.

Naari stepped forward, hand on her dagger. "It's already begun."

Jengo nodded, his spirit staff humming. "This is the source. The final gate… it's forming."

Chausiki's eyes narrowed. "Do you feel that?"

Jacques did. A deep, thunderous heartbeat beneath the ground. Then it erupted. A shockwave blasted through the crater as the crystal spire cracked and split apart. From its core rose the gate—a swirling vortex of black and violet, framed by pillars of flame and bone.

A voice echoed across the valley. "You are too late."

Erazion emerged from the gate, his form more twisted than ever, his aura leaking shadow into the sky. At his side stood Abuthos, his flesh marked by searing glyphs of corruption. And then, as the earth split further apart, the gate's core opened, revealing a figure rising. The monstrous Dark Lord, Hassatan. Still bound in chains of scorched by spiritstone, his face bore a smile so malicious that it made even his servants tremble.

"So, this is the army of the Creator," he hissed. "So small. So broken."

Jacques stepped forward, light burning from his chest. "We are not broken. We are united."

Elohim's voice rang through every soul present. "This is your moment. Protect the Heart. Seal the gate. Or all shall fall."

The Spirit Accord answered Elohim's call. All of them mounted up and made their charge as the Battle for Kan'Moro's heart began. Chausiki unleashed twin cyclones of wind and flame, clearing a path to the spire. Naari and Kisha flanked the left ridge, engaging corrupted spirits spilling from the gate. Jengo raised protective barriers around the warriors as arrows of spirit light rained from above. Jacques met Erazion in the heart of the battlefield. Their blades clashed viciously; light energy against dark void energy.

"Your master will not rise," Jacques growled.

"He already has," Erazion hissed.

Meanwhile, Chausiki had reached the gate's base. She pressed her palms to the corrupted veins, her spirit singing as she channeled Elohim's light into the seal. Hassatan roared, his chains weakening. Jacques summoned every ounce of his spirit power—earth and sky, wind and flame—and struck Erazion down with a beam of radiant fury.

Erazion screamed as he was flung back, shattered and faded into the ground. With one final cry, Chausiki poured her soul into the seal. The gate imploded as new chains reformed around Hassatan, dragging him back into the void. Silence followed, then the crater filled with light.

The Heart of Kan'Moro pulsed once more—pure, whole, divine. Jacques and Chausiki collapsed into each other's arms, exhausted but victorious.

However, above them, the stars shimmered strangely. Elohim whispered, "The gates are closed… but the echoes of the First War are not yet done."

Chapter Eighteen:
The Light After War

The battle was over. The gate was sealed, the Heart of Kan'Moro whole once more, and the land—for the first time in ages—breathed peace. Sunlight filtered through the mist that once cloaked the sacred crater. The Spirit Accord stood in reverent silence as Elohim's presence faded into the breeze, its warmth still lingering in their souls. Jacques and Chausiki knelt beside each other on the restored crystal spire. They were exhausted in body, mind, and spirit, but unbroken.

Around them, warriors tended to the wounded, whispered prayers, and sang songs of victory. Naari helped Kisha to her feet. Both were bruised but grinning. Jengo sat cross-legged, recording new glyphs into the Book of Light, documenting what had occurred.

Chausiki rested her head against Jacques' shoulder. "It's over."

Jacques nodded. "For now."

She smiled. "But we won. Not just the battle… we won the future."

They shared a soft kiss, one not of urgency or sorrow, but of quiet joy.

In the days that followed, the Spirit Accord returned to the Grove of Whispers. There, a great gathering was held. Tribal leaders from all across Kan'Moro arrived to honor the heroes and bear witness to a new age. Together, they formed the Council of Unity, a governing body representing every tribe, built not on dominance, but of shared vision. Jacques and

Chausiki were crowned not as rulers, but as Guardians of the Accord, protectors of spirit and peace.

Children were told stories of the battle under the stars. Of how wind and flame danced as one. Of how light pushed back the shadow. And at the heart of the ceremony came a moment of silence, as Jacques and Chausiki stepped before the Spirit Tree to share their vows before the entire assembly of the unified tribes.

Jacques took her hands gently and spoke from the depths of his heart. "Chausiki… I have walked the world with sword and flame, but I never knew true purpose until I met you. Your courage gave me strength. Your love gave me hope. I vow to stand by your side through storm and stillness. I vow to honor your heart, your fire, your spirit for all the days I am blessed to breathe."

Chausiki's voice trembled with emotion as she replied. "Jacques… you saw me not as a rival, but as a soul worth fighting for. In you, I found light, not just in power, but in peace. I vow to carry your burdens as my own, to guard your spirit as fiercely as I guard our people, and to walk every step of this life with your hand in mine." Together, they turned to the gathered tribes.

"With Elohim as our witness," Jacques said.

"With all Kan'Moro as our family," Chausiki added. "We seal this bond in spirit, in soul, and in love."

They embraced. And then they kissed.

A brilliant light descended from the sky, bathing the grove in golden warmth. Elohim's voice echoed over the land: "You have restored balance. You have redeemed what was broken. Let the Lightbearers rise not as warriors… but as peacekeepers of My creation. I am proud of you, my children.

Let the world remember your love and let your legacy shine brighter than the stars."

And so the light remained. The Spirit Wells glowed with harmony. And though the echoes of the First War still stirred in forgotten corners of the world, for now… peace had come, and love had endured.

Epilogue:
The Legacy of Light

Three years later…

The lands of Kan'Moro thrived like never before. Where once there were battlegrounds, there were now gardens, spirit sanctuaries, and places of learning and healing. The Spirit Accord had grown into a new civilization, one where the wisdom of the tribes flowed together like rivers joining a sea. At the heart of it all stood Ndavuu'Rae City, Mji wa Umoja, the City of Unity, where the Great Spirit Tree rose from the earth like a beacon and its silver-greenish leaves rustled in harmony with the wind; its roots entwined through the foundations of peace.

In the palace gardens beyond the Tree, laughter echoed. Jacques stood with his arms crossed, pretending to be stern as his son, Tariq, darted through the flowered path with a spirit-flame dancing at his fingertips. Beside him, Ayanda spun in a spiral of wind, giggling as petals scattered around her like confetti.

"Careful," Chausiki warned playfully from the terrace, a baby sling resting over her shoulder and a scroll in her other hand. "If you knock over the altar pots again, your father will have to repaint the whole garden."

Jacques smirked. "Let them try. It's tradition."

Tariq and Ayanda ran up to them, breathless, eyes glowing faintly with spirit energy. "Did we do it right?" Tariq asked.

"You did it with heart," Jacques replied, kneeling. "And that is always right."

Ayanda tugged at Chausiki's robe. "Mama, can we help at the gathering tomorrow?"

Chausiki nodded. "If you promise to listen as much as you speak."

They both shouted, "Promise!"

That evening, as stars returned to the sky, Jacques and Chausiki sat side by side beneath the Spirit Tree, their children curled up beside them. A gentle breeze stirred.

The voice of Elohim, soft and familiar, spoke once more: "From love, you built peace. From unity, you shaped the future. And from your legacy, others will rise. Not to rule, but to guide."

Jacques took Chausiki's hand. "They'll carry it on, won't they?"

She rested her head on his shoulder. "They already are."

Above them, the constellations formed a new symbol—a radiant spiral wrapped in flame and wind. The symbol of the Lightbearers as the symbol of a world forever changed. And, in every corner of the vast territories, from the highest mountain to the deepest forest, the message remained: The tribes were no longer many, they were are all one. They were now and forevermore known as the unified tribes of Kan'Moro.

TERRITORY OF THE
UNIFIED TRIBES
OF KAN'MORO

THE CHUI

THE DUMAJA

THE VODAI

N'DAVUU CITY

THE QUAAMATI

GREAT SEA

AZUURIIC
MHATU